SEAT 30

By Dan Armstrong

Seat 36

Chapter 1: Diagnosis

Chauncey Moore sat in the antiseptic glow of the examination room, the doctor's words still hanging in the air between them.

"Six months, at most." He'd closed her file with quiet finality. "The cancer has progressed too far for treatment."

She watched his face, searching for something—hope, perhaps, or at least regret—but found only the practiced neutrality of a man who had delivered this sentence hundreds of times before.

"What should I do?" The question felt small in her mouth, childlike.

The doctor's expression softened slightly. "Go home. Sleep in. Eat whatever you love. Have chocolate for breakfast. Nothing will change the outcome now—the life you have left is entirely yours." He paused at the door. "Take a train ride. Travel somewhere you've never been. It might clear your mind, refresh your soul."

Then he was gone, leaving her alone with the thundering silence of her mortality.

The fog at the train station clung to the ground like spectral fingers, swirling around Chauncey's ankles as she followed the faded yellow lines painted on the cobblestones. A week had passed since her diagnosis, a week of sleepless nights and frantic research.

That's when she'd first heard the whispers about Car 93.

They said only one person had ever returned from riding in that particular car—a man who claimed he'd been transported to 1852 and faced something called the Mediator of Life. Some called it a myth, others a scam, and a few believed it was something far more dangerous. But to Chauncey, with death already tracking her like a patient predator, danger had lost its meaning.

The station was eerily quiet for midday. No bustling commuters, no announcement boards flickering with arrivals and departures. Just fog and silence, broken only by the distant call of a single voice.

"Only one more ticket. One more ticket."

The ticket booth appeared through the mist—a narrow wooden stall with a pale glass window. Behind it sat a man wearing an oversized conductor's hat that cast shadows across his features.

"Are you riding today?" he asked when she approached.

Chauncey's throat tightened. Was she really doing this? "Yes, please. One ticket."

The man's booth seemed impossibly small, with no visible door or opening. His long, thin fingers slid a paper ticket beneath the glass.

"The train is boarding soon, ma'am. Car 93, straight away, behind you."

She turned to see the number "93", emblazoned in bold black letters on a gleaming red train car that hadn't been there moments before. When she looked back to ask how long the journey would take, the booth was empty, the man vanished without a sound.

A whistle pierced the fog—mournful, almost human in its cry. The train shuddered to life, metal groaning against metal. Chauncey clutched the ticket, suddenly afraid. But what was there to fear now? Death had already marked her. Whatever waited in Car

93 couldn't be worse than the slow decay promised by her disease.

She climbed the metal steps—one, two, three—just as the train began to move.

Chapter 2: Car 93

The interior of Car 93 stole her breath.

Curved ceilings draped with rich burgundy fabric arched overhead. Miniature crystal chandeliers cast prisms of light across the narrow corridor. The walls were paneled with polished mahogany, warm and gleaming in the emerald glow that filtered through stained glass windows. Heavy velvet curtains, held back by braided gold cords, framed each window like royal garments.

Chauncey moved unsteadily down the aisle, one hand trailing along the backs of plush green seats mounted on brass swivels. Each chair looked like a throne, designed for comfort and importance.

Her ticket read: Seat 36.

"Thirty-six," she whispered. "My age." A coincidence, surely.

It was only after she settled into her assigned seat, feeling the luxurious fabric embraced her like an old friend, that she noticed what should have been immediately apparent. The car was empty. Not a single other passenger occupied any of the dozens of ornate seats.

The last ticket on a full car, the booth man had implied. But she was alone.

The train's whistle sounded again, no longer merely mournful but keening like a soul in torment. The sound raised goosebumps on her arms. The train lurched, picking up speed, wheels clicking rhythmically on the tracks.

Thirty-six months. Thirty-six weeks. Thirty-six days.

The words came unbidden to her mind, keeping time with the wheels.

"Only one more ticket. One more ticket," she heard the porter say in her memory. "Why would he lie? Why would he pretend that the ride was sold out – only ONE more ticket?"

And just as she asked the question in her mind, a voice sounded at the end of the car. A narrow door opened and closed with a loud click. It was a conductor clad in 19th-century garb, spectacles on his nose as he looked over the rims. His hat, round at the top but with a firm brim, was angled to hover over his face.

"Tickets! Tickets!"

She shuddered for a moment. She was alone. "Why would he ask for tickets in the plural sense?"

He shuffled closer as the train wiggled, brokering the tracks with an unnatural aplomb. "TICKETS!" He walked closer, touching the curved ceiling on either side to keep his balance so as not to tumble. He tilted his head to see the passenger in a slump of worry. He smiled and stepped a chair and a half away.

"Ah, Chauncey, it's you. I've wanted to meet you."

Chauncey stared in disbelief. She had never uttered her name to anyone, not the porter, and there had been no one else until now. He repeated his request, "Ticket?"

Chauncey gripped the ticket between her thumb and forefinger, shaking. She lifted the piece of paper toward the conductor. He reached forward, stamped it continuously, and sat across from her.

"We need to talk."

Chapter 3: Roots

Chauncey remembered her childhood vividly. Her grandparents were devoted Democrats who cherished the idea of a government that extended a helping hand to the poor and needy. The Vietnam War began to shape their understanding that the world's problems were far larger than those of a single nation. However, the atrocities of war deeply troubled their souls. They turned away from the horrors of conflict and instead channeled their passion into the reverence for creation. They found beauty and worth in every living thing: the sparrow, the squirrel, and even the soil, which they mourned for its dwindling promise for the future.

A promise garden was planted to demonstrate the potential of honoring the soil and embracing the role of a steward of the earth. Each summer, Chauncey was summoned by her grandparents to their tiny homestead nestled on a hillside, far from the burgeoning city. There, she learned to watch the birds, water the plants, and nurture what remained of the receding forests. Enamored by their contentment and frugality, she nonetheless yearned for the exciting life of city lights, the curiosity of boys, and the quest to find "true" love among the myriad choices despite their eventual shallowness and somber consequences.

The conductor reminded her of her grandfather. He was serene, stoic, and stern when he peered over his goggles to make eye contact.

"Well, Chauncey, you bought a ticket," he said with a degree of certainty as if he wasn't surprised but wanted to hear her reason.

"I did." She looked straight ahead at the kindly old man. "I'm going to die, and..." she paused. How could she be so vulnerable to a stranger? Despite feeling safe, she summoned the courage to speak on this new journey.

"I have 180 days to live. Well, maybe 100 days, and then the rest are not living; rather, they are suffering the sorrow of breaking down from lucidity to the fuzziness of uncertainty. I want to make sure I..." she paused to collect her thoughts—though they raced about, she felt safe sharing intimate details of her life. "I want to make sure I know WHY I even lived!"

He nodded from the chair across from her. "Chair 36," he said.

She nodded back, "Yes, chair 36! I was surprised that I AM 36, and of all the chairs in this car, I bought a ticket for chair 36! How does that happen?"

The porter smiled. "There's no mistake. Everything is as it should be."

"So, that's it. I'm going to die regardless of riding on this train?"

"Everything is as it should be. In the course of your search, you bought a ticket, and it was for this seat, number 36." He placed his hands on the arms of the chair and gripped them tightly. "Do you trust me?"

She thought it an odd question yet conceded with a quick answer, "For some reason, yes. You remind me of my grandfather."

He chuckled. "I am getting older, and I forget that detail!"

"I'm sorry," she said.

"Ha! Don't worry. I know my gray hair, though a crown of glory is a sign to anyone younger that I am old. Within"—he paused and pointed to his chest—"I am the same young man who boarded this train when I was a lad."

Chauncey blew out a puff of air. "Yeah, me too! Only I keep thinking I'm 18 and just graduated from high school." She looked past the old man and saw the back of an old red barn. A large advertisement with words painted in yellow and framed in a black box read – "Olaf's Clothier – Expert Shirts – Fair Prices. $2.00."

She mouthed the words as she read them. The conductor knew the rail well and the sights to be seen. "You need some new clothing?"

Chauncey seemed embarrassed. "I'm sorry. I didn't mean disrespect. The sign on the barn caught my eye."

The old man chuckled, "It was meant to do so. Only the passengers on the train ever see Olaf's ask for business." He paused and waited until the barn was out of sight. "Do you know why Olaf advertised on that old barn?"

"It makes sense, I guess. Everyone is looking out the window as we leave the station."

He nodded. "Yes, but why do we look out the window? Why not stare at our hands or read a newspaper?"

Chauncey smiled, "Read a newspaper? What's that? I would think people are too busy scrolling on their cells."

The porter leaned back in his chair. It swiveled as the train shuffled on the steel guides. His eyebrows, thick as they were, performed a double act of confusion. Furrowed together, they almost touched at the height of his nose. "What?"

"Scrolling! We focus our eyes on a two-inch by five-inch screen." She nodded to see if he agreed.

He shook his head. "I have never heard of this word, 'scrolling'. This is from your time, yes?"

Chauncey breathed in deep and slowly let out a long exhale. She looked through the train windows again. Time seemed to slow down. She felt an uneasy sense of panic and, in equal measure, a sense of wonder about what was about to happen.

Open fields, grazing cattle, and not one utility pole in sight. "Wait a minute." She shot a quick breath out. "Where are we?"

The porter tilted his head. "You know where we are. You don't know 'when' we are."

She swallowed hard as she thought about standing from her chair and running to the door where she entered. They had yet to travel far. The train was moving at a snail's pace. She could jump and roll into a bank of grass as she had seen done in an old movie. Yes, that is what she would do. She would walk from there. Follow the tracks to the barn and walk another few hundred yards, maybe more. The old coot doesn't know what a cell phone is. He's playing a mind game!

"Chauncey!" he broke her internal dialogue. "If you jump off the train now, you can never go home," he shook his head left and right, "and you will never get to your destination either." His words were strangely comforting, the tone of a caring father.

"Okay, okay," she muttered, "a dream. That's what this is. I'm in a dream, and all I have to do is wake up." She began to lick her lips and was determined to fight the cloak of sleep. She closed her eyes hard and imagined a second before they would open that she would wake up on a train ride with passengers chatting about and pointing out the windows. Indeed, she felt sorry for herself and just wanted to be alone. The train ride recommendation was therapeutic; her doctor said, "It will clear your mind and refresh your soul."

She opened her eyes. The porter was gone. She could see the same scenery straight ahead and outside the windows – nothing had changed. And then she heard the voice. "Would you like to follow me?" It was the porter. She froze, and her skin shimmered with cold chills. He was standing at the door to the next car. "We will travel toward the engine where the smell of coal is stronger, but the sights are new and fresher."

Chauncey swiveled chair 36 toward the voice and stood up. Before she took one step, she asked, "Okay, Mr. Porter, 'WHEN' are we?"

He chuckled, looked over his spectacles, and said, "1852."

Chapter 4: Lesson One

"There's a reason the advertisement on the barn caught your attention." The porter squinted to see Chauncey's reaction. "The $2.00 price tag, right?"

She smirked before answering, "Yes. Who sells shirts for $2.00? That's an absurd price, especially if it's painted on a barn. It's not like it's on a digital billboard."

The old man quirked back, keeping his eyes trained on hers. "You and that language, such words I've never heard."

"Oh yeah … that's right! We're in the year 1852!" she remarked sarcastically.

The porter opened the door to the balconies between the two moving cars. He turned around and tilted his head, his chin doubling over his collar where a red necktie blossomed like a flower against a white shirt and emerald felt jacket. "It is becoming a more common occurrence."

"Common occurrence?" Chauncey belted out quickly. The rickety-rack of the train tracks drummed a steady rhythm with an occasional jolt as the hitches holding the cars together slid back and forth, making no attempt to stay in harmony with the forward motion.

"When people of your period visit the train. You always think you have advanced in everything but always miss the one thing." He pointed up with his finger.

Chauncey felt a soft thud of guilt tapping on her chest. She was judgmental. She knew it, too. The man looked like he belonged in the past; his presence alone carried a demeanor of trust and rugged individualism long assigned to the great men of that period—Theodore Roosevelt came to mind. "I'm sorry, sir." She shook her head and briefly looked at the shifting platforms between the cars. "It's just that I..." She blew out a burst of air. "I don't have long to live. As my doctor said, I was told this train would be therapeutic for me. I don't know. It's not what I expected."

"The shirts! $2.00! Wasn't that a clue?" the old man asked.

Chauncey paused before responding. It was strange indeed. The paint was bright and not aged at all. "Are they only $2.00?"

The porter chuckled again. "I think Olaf is greedy. Last month his shirts were $1.50!"

Chauncey laughed and moved carefully ahead. The breeze between the cars was brief, but with it came a waft of air that seemed to cleanse her face. It was pure. Not just pure, she thought, silky smooth! For a moment, she closed her eyes. She could hear the door to the next car open as the one behind her slammed shut. But the aroma of the air was intoxicating. Instinctively, she pushed all the air out of her lungs, and with all her might, she sucked in the air as though it would be her last before plunging into a deep reservoir of water. Her hands were clasped around two posts on the edge of the balcony. The tapping of life, the strums of blood pumping from her heart, and the overwhelming message of peace were all around her. She could stay here, holding on to metal poles, breathing the purest air, listening to the song of instruments as they frolicked together in synchronicity. Even with her eyes closed, she could see the green pastures and how the white clouds wisped like blankets in their blue playground.

"Chauncey."

She could hear her name but was caught up in a rapture of delight, a peace that surpassed all understanding of anything she was living through and dying for.

"Chauncey."

An eerie whistle pierced the serenity. She slowly opened her eyes, and standing at the next door was a man she had not seen for ten years. He spoke her name again, and for the second time on the train ride, her skin shimmered with cold chills from her back to her neck.

"Daddy!" Her heart sank. Her chest pounded.

"Yes, honey, it's me."

Her father had been gone for ten years, yet he was on the train, on the next car balcony. He reached out. His hand was the same one she recognized when the paramedic had released their fingers from his wrist, trying to find a pulse. "He's gone." The words echoed in her mind.

"It can't be you, Daddy." Chauncey felt her eyes swell with the pressure of tears, her heart expanding from within. The poles she was holding on to turned wet. Her hands were sweating, and she slipped away from them, wiping her hands on her hips. Her throat tightened.

"Take my hand, Chauncey. We are going into the next car to talk."

Her last memory of him was not his voice, but his face and his hand that had lain motionless by the side of a sofa from a life of despair. She reached forward, stepped over the thin space between two moving cars of the train, and took his hand. The door of the car opened, and the two passengers entered together.

The car they entered was not a first-class car. Chauncey had stepped out of. The carpeted floor was gone. Instead, a strict hardwood floor creaked as the train drifted slightly from side to side. The ceiling was flat and had no emotional gifts to give, save perhaps one of steadfast purpose. The walls on either side of the windows still boasted the brown lacquered finish, giving a sense of continuity but lacking the richness of the previous car. There were no curtains with fancy yellow cords, only shades that could be drawn, and the ones that were drawn flapped against the sills with the curtness of angry wood against wood.

"Sit down, honey." The man released his daughter's hand and pointed to two chairs facing each other in front of a window. It seemed a storm had gathered quickly. The light in the cabin was shrouded by a layer of gray. The mood was dim. The first thing Chauncey noted after sitting down was the presence of other passengers a few sections away from her and her father.

She looked at him. He looked the same as the day they had covered his face with a blanket. "Why are you here, Daddy?"

He seemed confused at the question. He asked, "I was told you came on the train." He looked up at the boring ceiling and then at the dark billowing clouds that seemed to chase the train. "The porter told me you bought a ticket, and I asked him if I could have some time with you before you decide."

Chauncey's mouth dropped. "What decision? I haven't considered any decision. I just wanted to ride the train."

He nodded. "You don't know where this train takes you, do you?"

"Daddy!" She began to cry. "Why did you go? Why did you …" she stopped. The word she wanted to say seemed disrespectful to speak—suicide.

"That's why I am here, Chauncey. I am here because you will have a decision to make. I made mine." He looked to his left. Dark gray skies spilled from the heights, slapping the earth with rain and sadness. "I made a choice, Chauncey. It wasn't right for me to make that choice. I realize it now, but it's too late to go back. The train is moving and taking me to my destination."

Chauncey wept as she heard her father's voice. His words were righteous, absent of guile.

"I lost my way. I could not see. Everything around me was black as night. Fear gripped my heart. Lies filled my mind, and I began to believe them. I wish I could tell you, Chauncey," he bowed his head, "my world was bleak, sad, and all I wanted to do was sleep." Then, he looked up rapidly, his eyes filled with a fierce stare, and he screamed. "I became more alive the day I died!" He shrunk into the chair and collapsed into his lap. His body heaved with grief, his shoulders shaking while his hands covered his face in shame.

Chauncey breathed deep. Her lungs bulged as she watched her father. Eyes fixed, widened at the spectacle before her. A man she loved dearly, placed on a pedestal of worship, the hero of her childhood now crumpled in a heap of despondency. He had made a final act in weakness when all his strength had failed him. Her heart began to break, not for her loss but for the pain that broke him. The emotion of anger—he failed her as a father—was dissipating. The charge against him of being selfish—he was only thinking of himself—was being dismissed. He was a person, a spirit, and a soul living in a body that gave him breath and life for a time. He was burdened, tortured, and unprepared to fight off the ravages of evil forces he knew nothing of. His fight was not of the world he understood. Every bad word, every unforgiving thought she replayed in her mind for the last ten years vanished. She forgives the man who was labeled as her father and permits him to be forgiven.

The clickity-clack of the railroad tracks suddenly became more noticeable. A whistle blew in the distance. A mountain echoed back a ghostly reply. Her father lifted himself from his repentant heart.

"Chauncey, there is hope!" He wiped his eyes and sighed. "You have more time than you think you do. I was selfish. You are not."

He looked again at the passing scenery. The billowing clouds were whiter than before, and the rain was spitting a few drops and not shouting at the ground as it had before.

"The destination I chose is the decision I made. It is not the decision you have to make. I gave up on hope. You do not have to."

Chauncey looked across the space between them. At first, it seemed intimate, warm, and holy, but the longer she stared at her father's figure, he faded. A vapor mist swept into the car, causing a cool breeze and her father's shadow to vanish. But not before she heard the words in his voice, "Hope, you have hope! And, I have love for you."

She closed her eyes and felt tears stroll from her swollen eyes. Streaks of pain joined with strokes of joy. She had felt her father's pain and forgiven the weakness of his heart. The clenched fists of anger toward a man she loved opened to release him. He was free of condemnation, free of judgment, and free to be loved again for the man he was in her childhood and on the day of his death.

"Chauncey."

She sat still, eyes closed, holding on to her last vision.

"Chauncey." The voice pierced the quiet moment. Why would anyone interrupt what had just happened? She opened her eyes slowly. Several passengers were chattering in unintelligible conversations a few feet away. None of them would have known her name. Her focus sharpened. She looked out the window to see the dark gray clouds were gone. Rolling green hills of tall grass and a gleaming white church in the distance caught her eye.

"Chauncey." That voice again! She was agitated. "Chauncey."

She woke up from the moment of meditation. The porter was standing beside her. "We have another car to visit before your destination. Follow me." Without waiting for a response, he smiled and began to stumble along as the train wobbled. He turned back and looked at Chauncey, "Better not be late. This train is always on time."

Chauncey stood and followed the porter. She looked back at the seat where her father spoke his last words, “I have love for you”. She could see him, not his physical body but him, the soul who longed to make it right and could not. Her heart pumped in her chest and rested too. Her father was gone and yet he was now with her. He was forgiven, free, and, forever with her as the Daddy she remembered.

Chapter 5: Lesson Two

Tiny giggles jostled about in harmony with the train's movement. Little bodies, shoulders, and heads tenderly bumped into each other, joyous laughter erupting with each tussle as gravity and centrifugal force acting upon them without prejudice.

Chauncey first noticed the smell of crackers and milk and the breath of children who had recently consumed them. "What is this, Mr. Porter?" She also noted an obvious absence – parents!

"Oh, these are Children of the Sky." His smile was broad, and he shook his head from side to side, seemingly enjoying their endless joy and infectious laughter. "These gems are always my favorite. I love this car!"

Confusion was written on her face, and a tinge of disgust made her smirk.

"What's the fuss with you? They're not bothering you. I think you ought to sit and speak with a few of them. There," he pointed, "There's a free seat."

Her eyes followed his finger to a rowdy group of five children. Three filled the seats on one side and two on the other. The empty seat between the two was her only choice, not an appealing one. Chauncey stumbled toward the cacophony of noise and chaos, and as chance would have it, the train threw her violently into the chosen seat. She screamed, followed instantly by an outbreak of whoops and hollers by the gang of small passengers.

"Oh, you think that's funny, do you?" Chauncey's face transformed from a sullen grin to a full, tooth-bearing smile. Without a thought for propriety, she reached toward the little girl beside her, maybe five years old, and tickled her belly to strike back at the embarrassing moment that caused the cackles. The girl shrieked in bliss. No sooner had the little girl gasped with laughter than another child across from Chauncey swooned in and begged for the same attention, "Tickle me, tickle me!"

"My, my!" She laughed at the raucous and addressed the child leaning forward. "We have to be careful in our seats."

The child who had begged for attention leaped forward and landed comfortably on her lap. He burrowed in, wrapped his arms around her waist as best he could, and squeezed. Chauncey was surprised but accepted the innocent affection as a gift. The little body buried his head into her belly and held her tightly. She could feel a sense of fear but also a bond of trust. The child had an ounce of fear but a pound of trust. An overwhelming intention of pure motherly love filled her as she received the hug. All the sounds of exuberance that had clouded her ears seconds before were now silent. When she glanced away from the child, there was a mob of hands and heads, mouths, and rampant movement, but no sound could be heard—only the pulse from the child's heartbeat from his wrist around her belly. 'Thump - thump, thump - thump.'

"He is safe with you." The porter's voice sounded as he walked past her. He tapped the other children's heads as he walked through the gauntlet of frenzied activity. She gazed at the child's black hair. His skin was a few shades lighter than the roots of his scalp.

She closed her eyes and begged time to stand still as she inhaled an unwarranted, unconditional love from a stranger. "What is your name?" he asked. He didn't move but gave another endearing hug. "My name is Chauncey." He remained quiet and steadfast in keeping hold of his treasure. She stroked his hair, her fingertips delving deep through the thick mop to find his scalp. "It's okay." She wasn't sure why she said it. "I'll stay here for as long as you wish."

The porter called out, "Tickets! Tickets!" The train shuddered abruptly.

The boy, who had melted into her flesh, released his grip and shot to attention. He stood before her, tears in his eyes, and spoke without moving his lips. It was not possible for him to say all he did in the time allotted, from the call for tickets to his departure, but she heard every single syllable as if he had lived a lifetime in her care.

"My name is Tobias. I am 8 years old. My grandma did all she could to keep me safe from the monsters outside the house, but they were stronger than the walls of our home. I was hungry and just wanted a piece of her pumpkin pie. Getting out of bed after bedtime was against the rules, but I was hungry. I wanted a piece of pumpkin pie. Grandma didn't hear me when I tiptoed down the stairs. The cat did and meowed a loud alarm, but Grandma was tired. She worked all day and sometimes at night so I could eat, and I loved her pumpkin pie. The lights were off, but I knew the way. I slid my hands along the stairway wall and measured my steps from the bottom of the stairs to my favorite room—the kitchen and the refrigerator where she put the pie, the pumpkin pie. I opened the door and smiled because I knew I was about to taste the best pumpkin pie in the whole world. And that's when I heard the noise. I should have stayed beside the refrigerator, but the noise…I had to know. The front window beside the door was really big. When I pulled the curtain back, the noise happened again. The biggest punch I ever felt hit me hard. I fell to the floor and for a moment, I thought Grandma would be mad. I crawled to the kitchen so she would know I just wanted some pumpkin pie. I was found on the floor of her kitchen the next morning."

Chauncey's mouth gaped. Her breath froze at the telepathic communication. His tears dripped from his cheeks and dropped to the floor. The collision of salt water on the hardwood floor thundered an explosion of emotions.

She wanted to shield the boy from further harm. He was destined for eternal care.

She wanted to scream for justice. He was about to receive the riches of Heaven.

She wanted to mourn the future of a soul who had not lived to the fruition of his dreams. He was giving his all to a stranger who was willing to receive who he was without prejudice.

The train came to an abrupt halt. Tobias stood erect like a soldier serving his duty with honor. The porter called out, "Tickets."

Chauncey stood and stepped protectively between herself and the child, intending to keep him safe in the car with her. Instead of hiding behind her, he gently pushed her away. "Let me pass, dear sister." Stoically, he spoke, "I am free, forgiven, and forever."

The words echoed those her mind had given her father as he passed from one car to another. Her father was forgiven, free, and forever with her. Now, the small boy who had lived a life of only eight years was the same. He would always be with her. His chocolate brown eyes melted her heart as he pressed past her and handed a small paper ticket to the porter. The porter took it, tucked it in a vest pocket, patted the boy on his shoulder, and watched him disembark with the eyes of a grandfather.

Though he whispered, his words could be heard. Chauncey began to weep. The porter said, "Child, receive your inheritance."

A bright light surrounded the railroad car. All the children became still and shielded their eyes. Tobias stepped out of the car, onto the platform, and as he took a step off the train, he vanished into a glorious brilliance of colors and symphonious sounds of an angelic chorus. Such beauty to behold and yet horror to the unprepared.

"Porter!" Chauncey screamed, "He did nothing wrong. Why has the innocent fallen?"

The light that had blinded her and the children began to fade. The muted moment was soon replaced by mischievous shouts and the playful chatter of children who knew nothing but wonder in a world of pain.

"Every soul plays a role, that's all I can say. I do not question the tracks of time. The chairs all have numbers and so do we. A life is born; another life passes on but never in the same measure. Although," the porter injected his personal philosophy, "it appears to me there is a line for each stop along the way. One cannot ask to be placed ahead or behind another ticket. But what do I know," he said with a smile. "I am just the porter, a guide. One passenger who returned called me a Mediator of Life and another the Doctor of Death. Which title I bear, I suppose, lends credibility to the ticket holder."

"Returned?" Chauncey asked. "What does that mean? We all return, don't we?"

Chauncey felt a tap on her elbow. "Want to play a game?"

She looked down to see a red-headed girl with freckles on either side of her nose and deep green eyes framed by a broken pair of glasses. Chauncey shook her head. "I don't want to play a game, Honey. Are you okay?" She leaned closer and saw maroon streaks on the girl's face, a sign of cuts, and a murky blue shadow under each eye. "Honey, wait, what happened?"

The little girl smiled and traipsed away. Chauncey noticed stains of dirt on her back. The porter spoke, "She's a wonderful little lady, isn't she?" He paused and pinched his lips. "The anger of someone she trusted could not be caged, and now the cage they live in cannot be broken, only their heart—but that is something she will never see."

Chauncey looked over the car of restless children; their heads bobbing up and down with the train's movements, their excitement for their own destination palpable. Each had a story, a song, a life cut short by someone else's foolish behavior. Chauncey asked quietly, "How many more stops for these little ones?"

The porter sniffed hard and sighed, "This car never seems to get emptied. Every time one gets off, two or more climb aboard. Damn the wars, the egos of men who need to take land, riches, and the lives of children to fill their paltry purse."

It was the first time Chauncey saw the porter show sadness. He always seemed perky or serious, but never sad. "Innocence lost." She spoke.

"Innocence lost," the porter repeated in agreement. "If you wouldn't mind, dear, would you settle in for a while longer? Talk to the kids. Show them your love."

Chauncey nodded. She looked behind her and was startled by what she saw. The car she had entered not long ago and had walked only ten feet to find her seat was now a mile long behind her, filled with the chattering clatter of hundreds of thousands of children. Their faces were beaming with excitement and glowing with happiness; victims of selfish humans who traded the breath of their babies for the convenience of a lifestyle. An eerie whistle blew and echoed as it bounced off mountains in the distance. Suddenly, Chauncey was aware of children taking turns hopping onto her lap and sliding off. The train halted abruptly, ten giggling souls floated away, then hundreds at a time fleeted like lucent mists, escaping through windows like wisps of dust swirling in melodic tunnels of rhapsody. The rumbling of the heavy steel-grooved wheels jerked forward and then it happened again, and again. A slow slide into a station of bright lights and amplified music with no rhythm; only the resonance of color, anti-time, and comfort unknown to the limited finite spectrum of a temporal mind. Slippery moments of brief flesh against flesh brushed against her cheeks and chin, and as quickly as she could embrace any one of the gregarious children, one by one, they would slip away into the light. Her mind was filled with names she had never heard before—Abetta, Benalla, Oreana, Risha, Tamaroa, Izranu, Omanika, and Nemanaka. Thousands of whispers. Names of children the world had forgotten but were now etched in the mind of a woman, diagnosed with terminal cancer, who bought a ticket on a train.

Children, the currency of the mighty. She wept for the souls of children who were sacrificed in war, under the hand of anger, and the greed for self-improvement. She could not count the stops the train had made, but it seemed endless as if to count for the economies of man's egotistical thirst for power. Treacherous was the path of those who could not fend for themselves in the annals of history.

"Chauncey," a familiar voice said her name. She opened her eyes and lifted her torso from her lap. The car was quiet, the train had stopped. "I want to show you one more car."

She looked around at all the seats. They were empty. The walls, though finished with a lacquer of varnish, were stained with handprints of mustard, tomato sauces, and the smears of snot from the ones who had no way of cleaning the sickness from their body.

"Where have they gone?" Chauncey pleaded.

The porter looked around as if it were a mystery. "Hmm. I suppose they are home." And with that, he made his invitation. "We are stopped for a few travelers who wish to board. They say their tickets are paid in full. In the next car, that is. Would you follow me, please?"

Chauncey felt full of love for the spirits that had swished and swirled around her soul, whispering their names, their dreams, hopes, and hurts. She was blessed without measure as to the experience one could never imagine had they not bought a ticket on the train.

"You say their tickets are paid in full? Whatever could you mean? Are not all tickets paid in full?"

The porter chuckled, "Paid in full? Hmm. Is anyone's ticket ever really paid in full?"

She shook her head and took the steps toward the next adventure. The narrow door opened, Chauncey looked back at the vacant car that needed thorough cleaning, and said, "It's a mess!"

"Yes, and I wouldn't have it any other way. Too soon our lives will fade."

Chapter 6: The Elder Car

Three steps in the rumbling living room on tracks, and Chauncey felt serenity come over her. It seemed she had returned to the first car with all the luxurious comforts of first-class. The plush seats were soft lime green fabric, yellow tassels at the bottoms bumbled about, tickling the carpeted floor. Unlike the children's car, where every seat was leather—easily cleaned by the onslaught of endlessly sticky fingers - this car was well kept. The curtains were thick, a royal moss green. The ceiling seemed to dance with natural light from small, narrow horizontal windows that showered the space with a glorious luminous glow. It was as if this would be the most beautiful tour of the train's cars, and why not? The car was full of gray-haired people looking straight ahead.

Chauncey remembered the car with her father, the storm brewing outside, threatening a perilous trip, but here—here there was sunshine and love. Their heads didn't bobble to and fro like the children, but they did bend to touch each other in gracious, tender moments of affection.

"Porter, this car is so quiet," she whispered so as not to draw attention to her presence.

"This car is reserved for our most distinguished passengers. They appreciate the tranquility and the comfort it offers. It's a place where time seems to slow down, allowing one to savor each moment."

Chauncey nodded, her eyes wandering over the elegant details of the car. The soft hum of the train on the tracks added a rhythmic background to the scene, enhancing the sense of calm. As she walked further down the aisle, she noticed the passengers, all with silver strands of hair, engrossed in quiet activities. Some read books with worn covers, others knitted with slow, deliberate movements. A couple shared a soft conversation, their hands intertwined in a display of enduring love.

"I sense there is a question ruminating behind your eyes," the porter queried.

Chauncey turned to him, smiling softly. "No, thank you. I was just admiring the peace here. It's such a contrast to the other cars."

The porter nodded in understanding. "Indeed. Each car has its own unique atmosphere. It's part of the charm of traveling on this train, don't you think? Every compartment tells its own story. I suppose that is becoming clear."

She agreed, appreciating the diversity of experiences the train offered. Each car was a small world to itself, filled with its own set of memories and emotions. Here in another first-class car, amidst the plush lime green seats and the golden tassels, Chauncey felt a profound sense of belonging. It was as if she had found a small sanctuary, a place where she could pause and reflect amidst the journey.

Chauncey found an empty seat near one of the narrow windows and settled in, gazing out at the passing landscape. The fields and hills rolled by, bathed in the soft glow of the afternoon sun. She took a deep breath, letting the serenity of the moment wash over her.

For now, in this tranquil car filled with quiet whispers and gentle gestures, she could forget the chaos of the world outside, the memory of her father, and the impetus that brought her there – the cancer diagnosis.

Here, she was enveloped in a cocoon of comfort and peace, a rare treasure amid her travels.

Chapter 7: The Choice

As Chauncey sat quietly in the elder car, gazing out the window at the passing landscape, an elderly woman with silver hair and bright, knowing eyes took the seat beside her.

"You're pondering quite deeply," the woman said, her voice gentle but clear.

Chauncey turned, surprised by the intrusion into her thoughts. "I'm sorry?"

"I recognize that look," the woman continued. "I wore it myself once. The look of someone trying to make sense of their journey." She extended a hand. "I'm Eleanor."

"Chauncey," she replied, accepting the handshake. The woman's grip was surprisingly firm for someone her age.

"I know who you are, dear. We all do. You're the passenger in seat 36."

A chill ran down Chauncey's spine. "How do you know that?"

Eleanor smiled. "Because you're the one the porter has been guiding through each car. That doesn't happen for everyone, you know."

Chauncey glanced around the peaceful car full of elderly passengers. "What is this place? What's happening to me?"

"This train," Eleanor said, gesturing around them, "is the journey between moments of decision. Each car represents a different understanding, a different perspective. Car 93 is where souls come when they're at a crossroads."

"The porter told me we're in 1852," Chauncey said skeptically.

Eleanor chuckled. "Time works differently here. What matters isn't when we are, but what we choose to do with the time we have."

The train whistle sounded - less mournful than before, almost questioning its' purpose.

"I was told I have six months to live," Chauncey admitted. "Cancer."

"Ah," Eleanor nodded. "That's what brought you to the train. Tell me, what have you learned so far?"

Chauncey considered the question, thinking back through her encounters. "I've seen my father—he took his own life years ago. We, "she paused to find the words, "We found peace… with each other. And I've held children who died too young through no fault of their own."

"And what did those experiences teach you?"

"That..." Chauncey paused, organizing her thoughts. Her heart pounded. "That my father made a choice in his darkest moment, one he regretted. And that those children had no choice at all."

Eleanor nodded. "Two sides of the same coin. The burden of choice and the tragedy of having no choice."

"But what does that have to do with me? I didn't choose to get cancer."

"No," Eleanor agreed. "You didn't. But you're choosing how to live with that knowledge."

The train rounded a bend, and sunlight streamed through the windows, casting golden patterns across their faces from the frames of every window.

"When I was your age," Eleanor said, "doctors gave me three months to live. Heart failure, they said. Terminal and irreversible." She tapped her chest. "That was forty-two years ago."

Chauncey's eyes widened. "How is that possible?"

"It's not about how long you live, dear. It's about how you live deeply. The doctors weren't wrong about my condition, they were wrong about what defines a life." Eleanor leaned closer. "I didn't beat my diagnosis by denying it. I beat it by refusing to let it define me."

"What did you do?"

"I chose to LIVE," Eleanor emphasized each letter of the word. "Not just exist, not just wait for death, but to truly live. When I left the hospital, I didn't go home to die. I went home to plant a garden I might never see bloom. I wrote letters to people I'd never met. I started projects I knew I'd never finish."

She reached into her pocket and withdrew a small silver key on a delicate chain. "And I bought a ticket for this train, just like you did."

Chauncey stared at the key. "What's that for?"

"Car One," Eleanor said with a wink. "It's at the very end of the train, past all the other cars. Not many find it, because not many look for it."

"What's in Car One?"

"The future you choose," Eleanor said simply. "Not the future you believe circumstances have dictated."

The train began to slow, wheels screeching slightly against the tracks. Outside, a platform appeared, bathed in soft golden light.

"This is my stop," Eleanor said, standing. She pressed the key into Chauncey's palm. "Take this. When you're ready—truly ready—use it on the last door of the last car."

Chauncey clutched the key, feeling its weight. "But I don't understand what…" Her voice drifted.

"You will," Eleanor assured her. "Remember this: life isn't determined by circumstances but made by choices to LIVE. Your diagnosis is a fact, but it isn't your destiny, unless you choose it to be so."

Several of the elderly passengers rose as the train came to a complete stop. They gathered their belongings with unhurried grace.

"Where are you all going?" Chauncey asked.

Eleanor smiled. "Home. We've completed our journey."

As the doors opened, a golden light flooded the car. Eleanor paused at the threshold of the door; mechanical steps mysteriously unfolded that led to a glistening surface just outside the train.

"The difference between existing and living is choice, Chauncey. Choose wisely."

With that, she stepped onto the platform with the others, their silhouettes gradually dissolved into the brilliance. When the last passenger had disembarked, the doors closed, and the train began to move again.

Chauncey looked down at the key in her palm. Etched into its surface was a single word: "Choose."

The porter appeared beside her. "I see Eleanor gave you, her key."

"What is Car One?" Chauncey asked.

"It's not a 'what', but a 'when'," the porter replied. "It's the moment you decide to stop being defined by your circumstances and start defining them instead."

"Can you take me there?"

He nodded. "Follow me."

As they made their way through several more cars, each one emptier than the last, Chauncey felt a strange lightness building within her. The burden of her diagnosis seemed to lift with each step, not because it had disappeared, but because she was walking away from its shadow and toward something else.

They reached a door unlike any other on the train—sleek, modern, with "ONE" illuminated in shifting colors above it.

"This is as far as I can take you," the porter said. "The rest of the journey is yours to make."

Chauncey hesitated, key in hand. "What will I find on the other side?"

"That depends entirely on what you're looking for," he replied. "But I can tell you this: no one who passes through that door returns the same."

Taking a deep breath, Chauncey inserted the key into the lock. It turned with surprising ease, and the door slid open to reveal not another train car, but a vast, open space filled with countless doors of every description - some grand and ornate, others simple and wooden, some ancient, some futuristic, some barely more than curtains of light.

"What is this place?" she whispered.

Though the porter hadn't followed her through, his voice seemed to surround her. "These are the doors to all your possible futures - each one represents a way you might choose to live the time you have left, whether that's six months or sixty years." His voice echoed.

Chauncey stepped forward, drawn to a particular door—painted green, with a brass knob that reminded her of her grandparents' home. Through its window, she could see a garden where people of all ages worked together, planting and harvesting.

"My grandparents' promise garden," she breathed.

"One possibility," the porter's voice confirmed. She didn't see his face behind her, but she knew he was nodding his head.

Her eyes traveled to another door, behind which she could see researchers in white coats working in laboratories alongside patients receiving treatment.

"You could dedicate your remaining time to finding a cure," the porter suggested. "Not for yourself, perhaps, but for others who will come after you."

Door after door revealed different possibilities - traveling to places she'd dreamed of, teaching children, writing, creating, loving, living. But Chauncey noticed something remarkable: regardless of which door she examined, her reflection in its surface showed her vibrant and purposeful, not diminished by illness but enlarged by purpose.

"I understand now," she said. "It was never about which path I choose. It's about choosing at all - deciding to live fully no matter how much time I have."

She approached the green door of her grandparents' garden, feeling drawn to the legacy she'd once turned away from. As her hand touched the brass knob, a surge of energy coursed through her.

"Remember," the porter's voice said as she turned the knob, "the door is just the beginning. The journey continues on the other side."

"But this time," Chauncey said with newfound certainty, "I'm choosing the journey, not just letting it happen to me."

Brilliant sunshine washed over her face as she pushed the door open. The scent of rich soil and growing things filled her lungs. Voices called out in welcome. Before stepping through, she turned one last time.

"Thank you," she whispered.

The train whistle sounded in the distance—triumphant now, not mournful. Chauncey Moore stepped through the door of her chosen future, leaving behind the woman who had boarded Car 93 seeking the meaning of her existence. That question no longer mattered.

What mattered was that she had chosen to create meaning with whatever time remained.

And in that choice lay the freedom to truly live.

About the Author

Dan Armstrong is the author of *The Adventures of a Real Life Cable Guy,* a memoir reflecting on his career, and *Smart Dust – The Dawn of Transhumanism,* a science fiction novel inspired by real-world technology. His bestselling fantasy series, *The Chronicles of Elwic,* includes *The Temple of Wisdom and Truth* and its sequel, *Tales of Havenbrook.*

Dan has established himself across multiple genres with bestsellers including *What the Soil Remembers*, *The Blackboard Passage*, *Stop Petting the Burning Dog*, and *Being True to Your Purpose*.

He has co-authored two #1 bestselling books with Kyle Wilson International: *Think Big* and *Next Level Your Life*. Additionally, Dan contributed as a commentary author in the bestselling book *The Moral Compass*, written by Moe Rock, CEO of *The Los Angeles Tribune*.

Books by Dan Armstrong

Available on Amazon

The Adventures of a Real Life Cable Guy – Shorts stories – a memoir of a career

LONG READS (FICTION)

Smart Dust – The Dawn of Transhumanism

The Chronicles of Elwic – The Temple of Wisdom and Truth

The Chronicles of Elwic – Tales of Havenbrook

LONG READS (NON-FICTION)

Being True to Your Purpose

SHORT READS (FICTION)

The Blackboard Passage

What The Soil Remembers

Seat 36

The Book of Becoming

SHORT READ (NON-FICTION

Stop Petting the Burning Dog – 7 Uncomfortable Truths That Will Actually Change Your Life

Micro-Excellence – Small Steps – Big Changes

Your Unique Path – Defeating Comparison

COLLABORATION BOOKS

Think Big – Kyle Wilson International

Next Level Your Life - Kyle Wilson International

The Moral Compass – Moe Rock, Los Angeles Tribune

If you would like to purchase books in bulk – please email danarmstrongauthor@gmail.com

Made in the USA
Columbia, SC
20 April 2025